W9-CEI-393

The
Rooster Prince
of Breslov

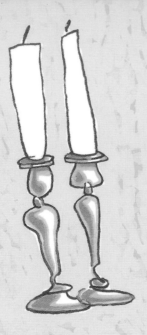

In loving memory of my
father, Harold Redisch
—A.R.S.

To the members of the
Jewish Artist Initiative
of Southern California
—E.Y.

Clarion Books
215 Park Avenue South, New York, New York 10003

Text copyright © 2010 by Ann Redisch Stampler
Illustrations copyright © 2010 by Eugene Yelchin
Title hand lettering by Leah Palmer Preiss
Designed by Christine Kettner
The illustrations were executed in graphite and gouache
on watercolor paper.
The text was set in Gararond.

CLARION BOOKS is an imprint of
Houghton Mifflin Harcourt Publishing Company.

www.hmhbooks.com

Manufactured in China

LIBRARY OF CONGRESS CATALOGING-IN-PUBLICATION DATA
Stampler, Ann Redisch.
The rooster prince of Breslov / by Ann Redisch Stampler ;
illustrated by Eugene Yelchin.
    p. cm.
  Summary: In this variation of a Yiddish folktale, a spoiled prince has a fit
and assumes the speech and mannerisms of a rooster until he is locked in a
room for seven days with a frail grizzled old man.
  ISBN 978-0-618-98974-4
  [1. Jews—Folklore. 2. Roosters—Folklore. 3. Folklore.] I. Yelchin, Eugene,
ill. II. Title.
PZ8.1.S7865Ro 2010   398.2—dc22
  [E]   2009033580

LEO 10 9 8 7 6 5 4 3 2 1

4500227781

The Rooster Prince of Breslov

by ANN REDISCH STAMPLER

illustrated by

EUGENE YELCHIN

CLARION BOOKS
HOUGHTON MIFFLIN HARCOURT
Boston / New York / 2010

I N BRESLOV, there lived a prince who had more than he wanted. When
he was hungry for a scrap of bread, he got a slice of cake dripping with honey.
When he asked for a raisin, he was given a silver bowl of candied plums. When his
eyes rested on a pony or a strudel or a bird's nest or a golden ball, it was bundled
up and brought to him before he even blinked.

One day, right in the middle of a lavish lunch he didn't want and barely touched, he cried, "Enough!"

With that, the prince jumped out of his chair, ripped off his clothes and shoes, and squatted on the marble floor.

"Buck-buck-buck," he clucked, scratching at the tiles with his toes and pecking at crumbs. Then, into the stunned silence of the banqueting hall, he crowed, "Cock-a-doodle-doo!"

C O C K A D O

Despite the best efforts of his royal parents, the prince would not get dressed or eat at the table or speak a single human syllable. The king and queen were at their wits' end. Finally, after a long week of clucking and cock-a-doodle-doos, the king offered a bag of gold to anybody who could cure his son.

O DL E DOO

First came a doctor with a satchel full of medicines. When he tried to dribble sticky drops onto the prince's tongue, the prince pecked his hand. "Cock-a-doodle-doo!" yelled the prince as he chased the doctor out the door, flapping his arms.

The king and queen were waiting anxiously in the corridor. "Your son has the most serious case of . . . um . . . uh . . . *roosterism* I have ever seen!" the doctor said. "Perhaps you'd better send for a magician."

The next day, a whole platoon of magicians arrived
to see the prince. They chanted spells and sprinkled their
potions onto the prince and the furniture too, but to no
avail. "Cock-a-doodle-doo!" cried the prince, and he
pecked at their legs until every sorry sorcerer had fled.

Before long, only one frail old man, all gray and grizzled, was left. He had no bag of medicine, no potions or pills, and when the queen peered up his sleeve, she saw no magic wand, only a skinny arm.

"Are you a doctor?" she asked. "Or a sorcerer or a magician?"

"I am not," the old man answered. "But if you give me seven days, and do exactly as I say, I promise I'll return a prince ready to rule the land."

"One week?" asked the king, eyeing him suspiciously.

"Believe me, bigger things have been accomplished in that time," the man replied.

"But will he be just as before?" the queen demanded.

"Well, not exactly," said the old man. But his wrinkled old face looked so wise, and the king and the queen were so desperate, that they agreed to provide all the odd things he asked for. Then they led him to the room where they had locked up the prince.

When the old man entered, the prince was pecking at kernels of corn that had been thrown onto the floor for him. "Cock-a-doodle-doo!" he raged, careening toward the old man.

"Cock-a-doodle-doo," replied the old man quietly. He pulled off his clothes, squatted down on the floor, and began to peck the corn as well.

The prince teetered to a sudden stop. "What are you doing?" he demanded.

"I am a rooster," replied the old man. "And I was a little hungry . . . do you mind if I share your corn?"

The prince had never shared anything with anyone before. He stared at the old man, his mouth open as wide as a bucket. "Do you know who I am?" he asked.

The old man kept chewing. "Of course I do," he said. "You are a rooster, just like me."

All day long, the old man hunched beside the prince, pecking and strutting and clucking in a friendly way. At night, when the prince went to sleep on the cold floor, the old man did the same.

The second day was exactly like the first: the old man and the rooster boy bucking and clucking and pecking at corn, side by side.

When the room grew dark, the old man pointed to two straw mattresses that had been slipped into the corner. "Cluck-cluck, what are those things?" he asked through a yawn.

"Buck-buck-buck!" replied the prince. "Those are beds."

"What are they for?"

"Buck-buck," said the prince. "For people to be comfortable when they sleep."

The old man waddled to one of the mattresses and looked at it longingly, rubbing his neck, which was stiff from his night on the floor.

"Why should humans have all of the comfortable beds while we roosters sleep on the ground?" he asked.

"You know," said the prince, "maybe a nice old rooster could sleep on it."

"You're right!" said the old man. He climbed onto the mattress and fell asleep.

When he awoke the next morning, the prince was fast asleep on the second mattress. The room was filled with the aroma of warm black bread. "Cluck-cluck," the old man said, pointing at a tray on the floor. "What's that?"

"Buck-buck," replied the prince, rubbing his eyes. "That is black bread."

"What is it for?" asked the old man.

"People eat it," explained the prince. "It's very tasty with butter when it's warm like that."

"Again for the humans!" clucked the old man.

"Buck-BUCK!" replied the prince, watching the old man try to chew a hard kernel of corn. "Maybe a hungry old rooster could eat just a bit of soft bread."

The old man took the warm bread and tore off a piece. "You're right!" he said, munching happily. "Why should people get all the tasty warm treats while we roosters gnaw on rock-hard corn?"

Soon the prince was squatting beside him, hungrily eating the rest of the bread.

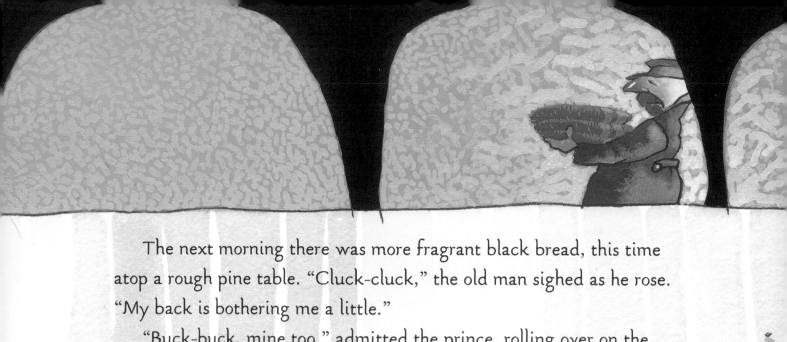

The next morning there was more fragrant black bread, this time atop a rough pine table. "Cluck-cluck," the old man sighed as he rose. "My back is bothering me a little."

"Buck-buck, mine too," admitted the prince, rolling over on the lumpy mattress.

"I see they have put the black bread on that thing," the old man said, "next to those other things, with all those legs. What are they for?"

"You mean that swayback table?" asked the prince. "That's for people to sit at when they eat. And the rickety chairs? They are what people sit on."

"Cluck!" muttered the old man, rubbing his back. "People again."

"Well!" said the prince, jumping up. "What harm would it do if an old rooster like you sat comfortably?"

At that, the old man climbed onto one of the chairs. "You're right!" he said. "Why should people get all the comfort when they eat, while we roosters have to strain our backs?"

After a few minutes, the prince climbed onto the other chair, and they ate their black bread seated side by side.

That night, the old man and the prince awoke with a start. Someone had thrown open the windows while they slept, and the autumn wind was whistling through the room.

"Cluck-cluck!" chattered the old man. "I am so cold!"

"BUCK-buck-BUCK-buck-BUCK!" The prince shivered in agreement.

As the first light of day filled the room, the prince saw a thin blanket folded neatly on the table. Too cold even to remember to strut like a rooster, he grabbed the blanket and wrapped it around the old man and himself. "This is a very scratchy blanket," he said, before the old man could ask. "People use it to keep warm."

"People this and people that," complained the old man. "How are we roosters supposed to keep warm?" The prince shut the window, and they spent the whole cold day with the blanket draped over themselves and their two chairs.

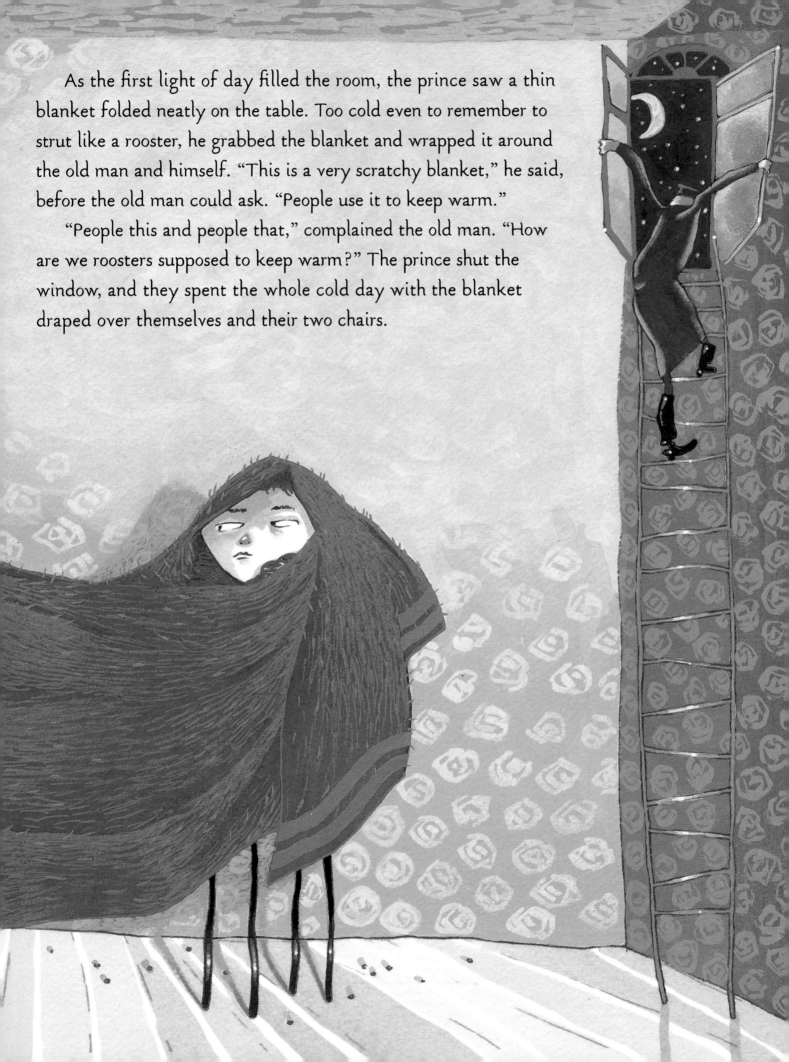

The sixth day, it was even colder. "What do people do when it is cold like this?" the old man asked. "Do they not have some clever way to keep themselves warm, unlike us unfortunate roosters?"

"Cluck-cluck-CLOTHES!" said the prince. He pointed to the piles of clothes he and the old man had discarded. "Why should an old rooster like you shiver all day long?" And they scurried to get dressed.

"This is delightful!" said the old man, squatting on the floor in his woolen trousers and his big black coat.

"BUCK-buck-*brilliant!*" replied the prince, happily buttoning the shirt he hadn't worn for weeks and pulling on his socks.

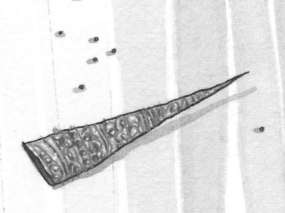

The seventh day, the old man and the prince woke up on the straw mattresses under rough blankets, stretched, and put on their warm clothes. They sat on their rough pine chairs, eating coarse black bread and clucking contentedly.

Just before nightfall, a beautiful braided challah, a pot of stew, a small jug of wine, candlesticks, and a silver cup were brought in and placed on the table.

"What is this?" asked the old man.

"This is a Sabbath feast!" replied the prince.

The old man rose to his feet. "Mmmmm, it feels good to stand up," he said. "For why should people light these beautiful candles when we poor roosters, squatting on the ground, cannot? Come help, young friend!"

Slowly, the prince stood up. Together he and the old man lit the candles and said the blessings, ate the challah and drank the wine.

When they had finished their meal, the old man spoke solemnly. "My friend," he said, "the week is done, and it is time for me to go home. How I hate to leave a fellow rooster behind in this place where roosters have no comfort and no warmth, no clothing and no Sabbath feast, and people have everything. What will become of you?"

The prince sighed.

The old man scratched his chin. "Well, you do look quite a bit like a person," he said. "In fact, you look exactly like the prince."

"I'm a rooster!" insisted the prince. "Can't you see the way I strut and crow and flap my wings and scratch the floor? Just because I slept on a mattress and ate at a table and put on these clothes—that doesn't make me a man."

"You're right!" replied the old man. "It's the way you treated a cold, hungry, achy old rooster that makes you a man. For it was you, Your Majesty, who wrapped me in a blanket and shared your Sabbath feast with an old traveler. It is lucky for you that you look like a man, for you have just become one."

The prince thought hard and long, and when he got up from his chair, he felt he was perhaps a little taller than he'd been before.

And that is how it happened that the prince grew up to be a fine king. And sometimes, when the sky was blue and the sun was high and he heard his own son whistling a tune, he almost forgot that he had ever been a rooster.

AUTHOR'S NOTE

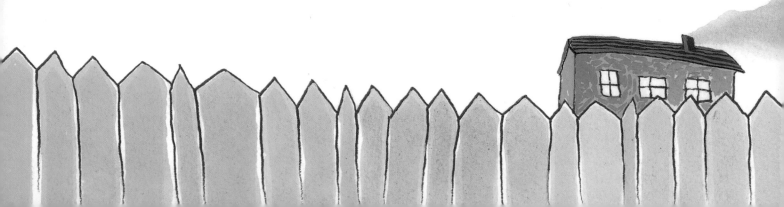

The TALE OF THE ROOSTER PRINCE is one of the best-loved Yiddish folktales. It has appeared in many versions in different lands, often with a lesson tied to the time and culture in which the bird boy finds himself. The message that is generally taken from Rebbe Nachman of Breslov's (1772–1810) early, spare version of this tale is that for a teacher to raise his student to the heights of spiritual ecstasy, that teacher must approach the student at the student's own level, no matter how low.

I see the rooster prince tale as a coming-of-age story that explores, with great humor and tenderness, the question of how to nurture a child so he or she will grow up to become a good person. In the story a confused and alienated boy becomes a man by developing *rachmunis,* or true compassion, and practicing *mitzvoth,* or good deeds. This lesson has meaning for him in the present, as well as for his adult self, who will carry forward the values of his culture. His stature as a prince suggests that all children, no matter how privileged, must go through this developmental process in order to become kings and queens—adults with moral authority in their families and communities.

My grandmother came to America from an impoverished village in eastern Europe, and she found the material comforts available in her new country overwhelming. When she told this story, her message was that growing in spirit and compassion was not exactly a by-product of the material splendor available to American children but emerged, instead, from honoring our human connections and sharing our traditions.